SACR Y0-BSC-247

Sacramento, CA 95814

08/21

WHOLE WIDE WORLD
GREAT WALL OF
CHINA

by Kristine Spanier, MLIS

Ideas for Parents and Teachers

Pogo Books let children practice reading informational text while introducing them to nonfiction features such as headings, labels, sidebars, maps, and diagrams, as well as a table of contents, glossary, and index.

Carefully leveled text with a strong photo match offers early fluent readers the support they need to succeed.

Before Reading

- "Walk" through the book and point out the various nonfiction features. Ask the student what purpose each feature serves.
- Look at the glossary together. Read and discuss the words.

Read the Book

- Have the child read the book independently.
- Invite him or her to list questions that arise from reading.

After Reading

- Discuss the child's questions. Talk about how he or she might find answers to those questions.
- Prompt the child to think more. Ask: The Great Wall is a symbol of China's history. What are some symbols of history where you live?

Pogo Books are published by Jump!
5357 Penn Avenue South
Minneapolis, MN 55419
www.jumplibrary.com

Copyright © 2021 Jump!
International copyright reserved in all countries.
No part of this book may be reproduced in any form
without written permission from the publisher.

Library of Congress Cataloging-in-Publication Data

Names: Spanier, Kristine, author.
Title: Great Wall of China / by Kristine Spanier.
Description: Minneapolis, Minnesota: Jump!, Inc., [2021]
Series: Whole wide world | Includes index.
Audience: Ages 7-10 | Audience: Grades 2-3
Identifiers: LCCN 2020027320 (print)
LCCN 2020027321 (ebook)
ISBN 9781645277385 (hardcover)
ISBN 9781645277392 (paperback)
ISBN 9781645277408 (ebook)
Subjects: LCSH: Great Wall of China (China)
Juvenile literature. | Civil engineering—China
History—Juvenile literature. | China—History—To 221 B.C.
Juvenile literature. | Walls—China—Design and
construction—History—Juvenile literature.
Classification: LCC DS793.G67 S695 2021 (print)
LCC DS793.G67 (ebook) | DDC 931—dc23
LC record available at https://lccn.loc.gov/2020027320
LC ebook record available at https://lccn.loc.gov/2020027321

Editor: Jenna Gleisner
Designer: Molly Ballanger

Photo Credits: Hung Chung Chih/Shutterstock, cover,
5; Sun Xuejun/Shutterstock, 1; chpua/iStock, 3;
Imagemore Co, Ltd/Getty, 4; junrong/Shutterstock,
6-7; FrankvandenBergh/Getty, 8-9; Peter Chafer/
Shutterstock, 10-11; Hungchungchih/Dreamstime,
12; real444/iStock, 13; Inzyx/iStock, 14-15; Mariusz
Prusaczyk/Dreamstime, 16-17; Tada Images/Shutterstock,
18; View Stock/Getty, 19; Xinhua/Alamy, 20-21; zhao
jiankang/Shutterstock, 23.

Printed in the United States of America at
Corporate Graphics in North Mankato, Minnesota.

TABLE OF CONTENTS

CHAPTER 1

FIGHT FOR CONTROL

There were many kingdoms in **ancient** China. They fought for control. They built walls for protection. Some were made more than 2,500 years ago! Qin Shi Huang won control. He became China's first **emperor** in 221 BCE.

Qin Shi Huang ····▶

He wanted to connect the walls. It took 10 years. More than one million people worked to connect them. It is now known as the Great Wall of China. It runs west to east in northern China.

Great Wall of China

The wall starts in Jiayuguan. It goes east to Shanhaiguan. It meets the Bohai Sea. Some call this part the Old Dragon's Head.

WHAT DO YOU THINK?

The Great Wall has many names. Some call it the Long Wall. Others call it the Earth Dragon. What would you call it? Why?

Bohai Sea

The wall helped protect China. How? It kept northern **invaders** out.

It was built with stones and **adobe**. Each new leader added to the wall. It is now more than 13,000 miles (20,920 kilometers) long.

DID YOU KNOW?

The Great Wall is the longest **structure** made by humans!

Great Wall
of China

brick

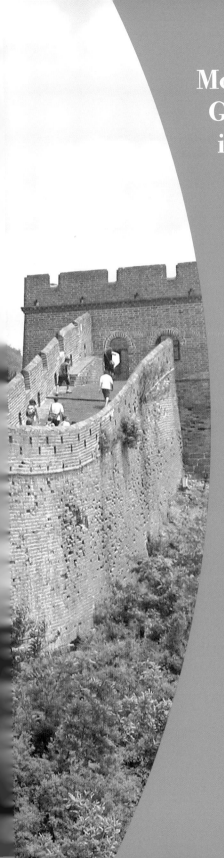

Mongolia is just north of China. Genghis Khan was the leader in 1211 CE. The average height of the wall is about 25 feet (7.6 meters). But Genghis Khan's soldiers got past. Mongolia controlled China until 1368.

The Ming **Dynasty** lasted from 1368 to 1644 CE. During this time, workers made the wall stronger. They used granite, brick, and limestone.

CHAPTER 2

PARTS OF THE WALL

Towers stood at high points along the wall. Soldiers sent messages to one another from them. How? They lit fires and lanterns. They used smoke **signals**, too. Sometimes they fired cannons.

tower ......▶

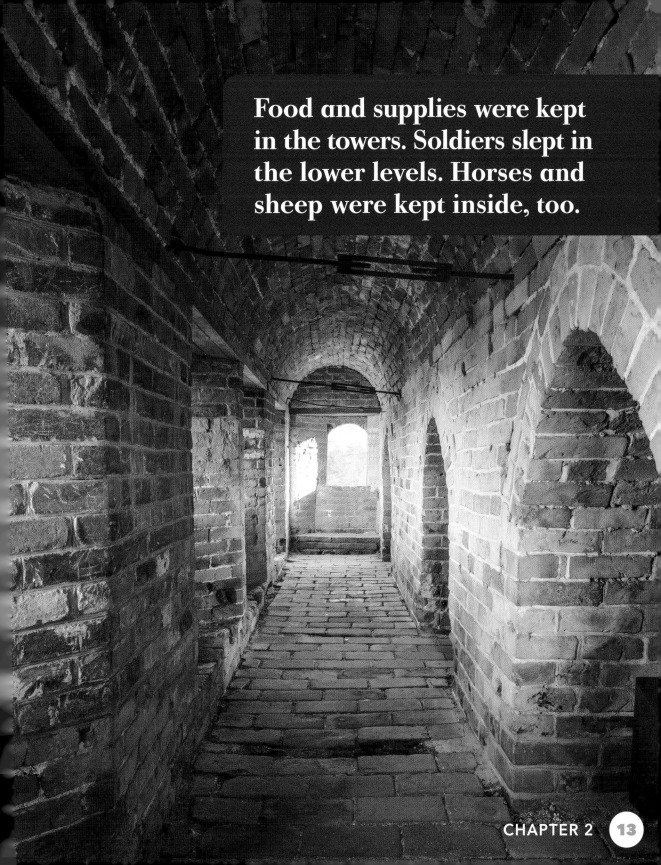

Food and supplies were kept in the towers. Soldiers slept in the lower levels. Horses and sheep were kept inside, too.

pass

The wall was on a **trade route**. It was called the Silk Road. Passes were built into the wall. Soldiers allowed people to get through with **goods**.

WHAT DO YOU THINK?

Passes helped control who moved in and out of China. Do you think walls should control where people can and cannot go? Why or why not?

Parts of the wall are about 19 feet (5.8 m) wide. People and horses could walk along it. **Waterspouts** protected the wall from rain.

TAKE A LOOK!

The wall has many features. Take a look!

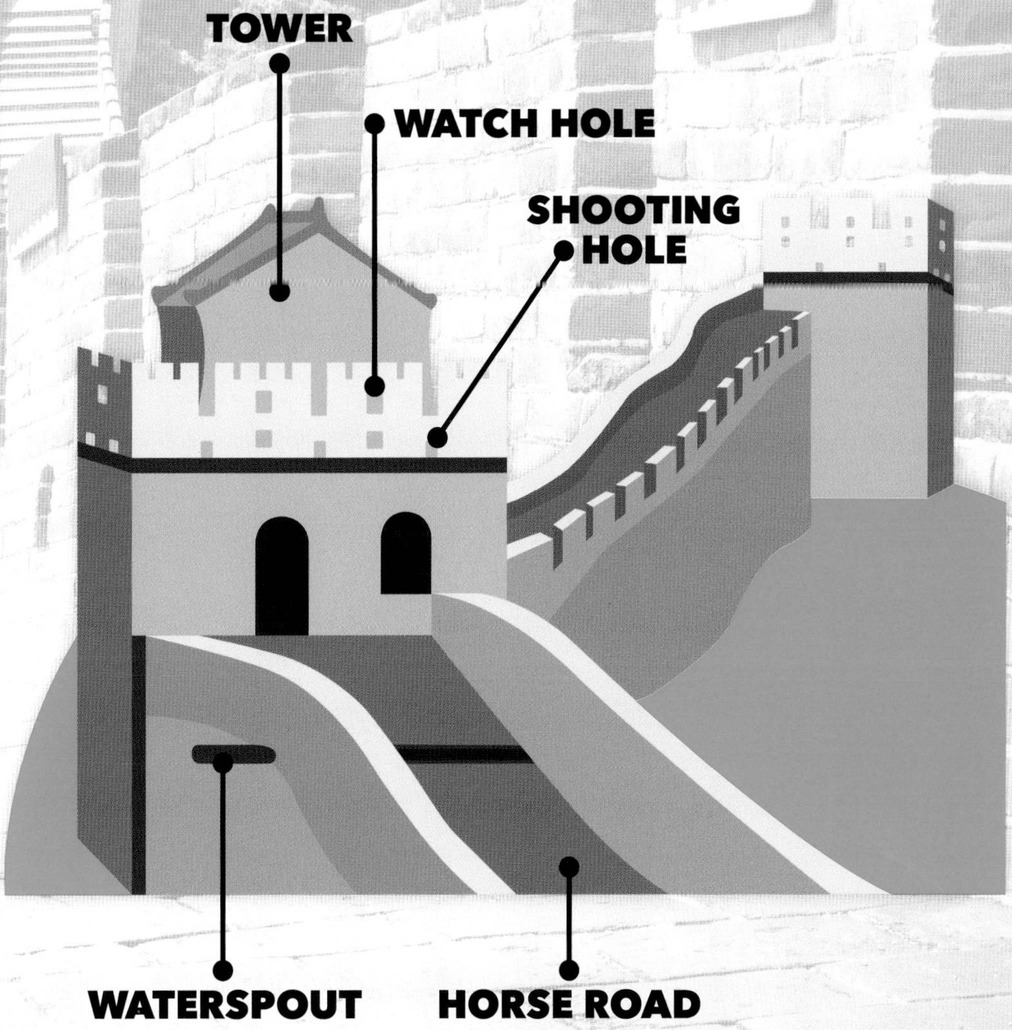

TOWER

WATCH HOLE

SHOOTING HOLE

WATERSPOUT

HORSE ROAD

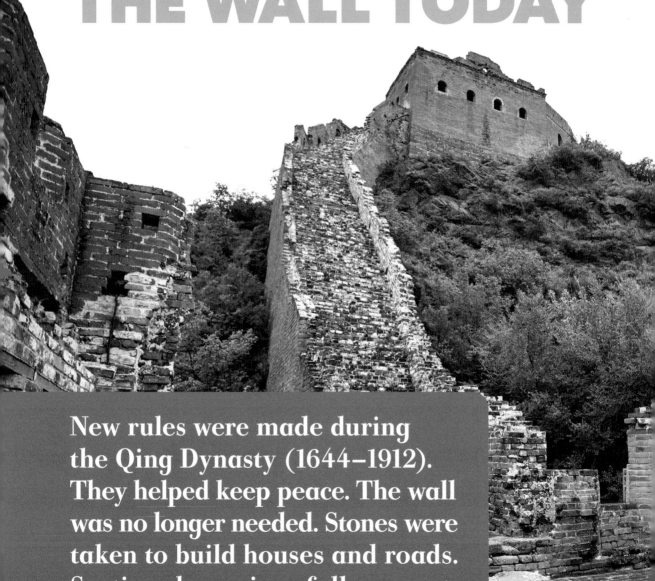

CHAPTER 3

THE WALL TODAY

New rules were made during the Qing Dynasty (1644–1912). They helped keep peace. The wall was no longer needed. Stones were taken to build houses and roads. Sections have since fallen apart.

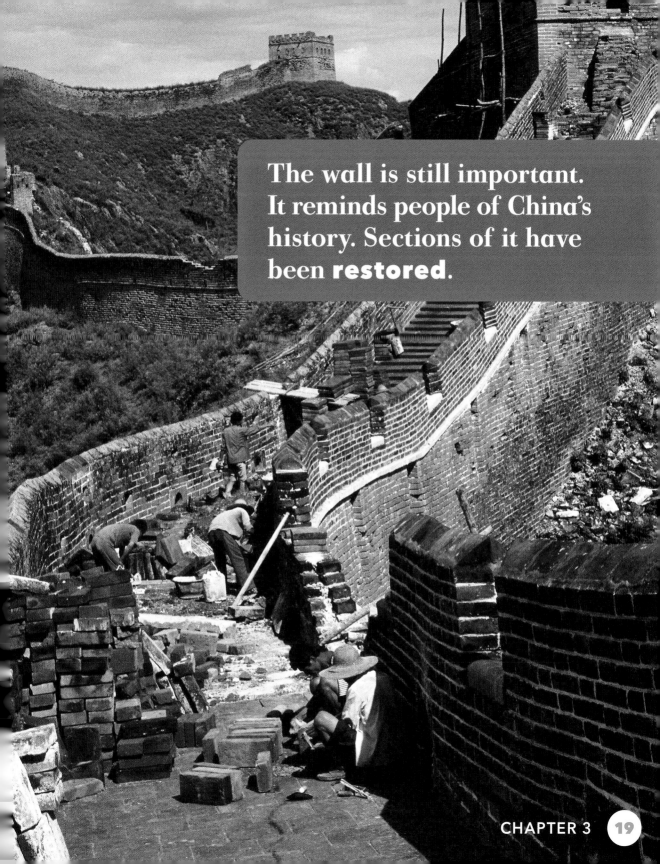

The wall is still important. It reminds people of China's history. Sections of it have been **restored**.

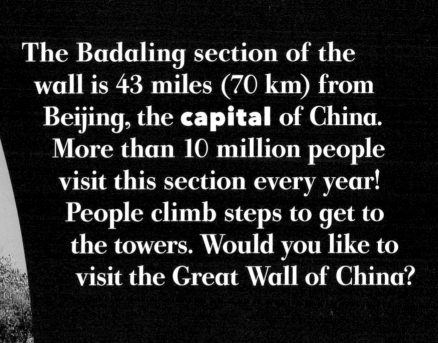

The Badaling section of the wall is 43 miles (70 km) from Beijing, the **capital** of China. More than 10 million people visit this section every year! People climb steps to get to the towers. Would you like to visit the Great Wall of China?

QUICK FACTS & TOOLS

AT A GLANCE

GREAT WALL OF CHINA

Location: Northern China

Length: 13,170 miles (21,195 km)

Years Built: 700s BCE to 1600s CE

Past Use: boundary marker and protection

Current Use: tourist site

Number of Visitors Each Year: around 10 million during peak season (from April to October)

GLOSSARY

adobe: Bricks that are made of clay mixed with straw and dried in the sun.

ancient: Belonging to a period long ago.

capital: The city in a country or state where the government is based.

dynasty: A series of rulers belonging to the same family.

emperor: The ruler of an empire.

goods: Things that are sold.

invaders: Armed forces sent into a place to occupy or control it.

restored: Brought back to an original condition.

signals: Signs that send messages or warnings.

structure: Something that has been built.

trade route: A route or path along which people travel to buy and sell goods.

waterspouts: Pipes or openings for carrying water away.

INDEX

TO LEARN MORE

Finding more information is as easy as 1, 2, 3.

1 Go to www.factsurfer.com

2 Enter "GreatWallofChina" into the search box.

3 Choose your book to see a list of websites.

FACT SURFER